FOLLOW ME, FLO!

JARVIS

FOR MY JENNA x

First published 2020 by Walker Books Ltd, 87 Vauxhall Walk, London SE11 5HJ • © 2020 Jarvis • The right of Jarvis to be identified as the author and illustrator of this work has been asserted by him in accordance with the Copyright, Designs and Patents Act 1988 • This book has been typeset in Bodoni Antiqua T • Printed in China • All rights reserved. No part of this book may be reproduced, transmitted or stored in an information retrieval system in any form or by any means, graphic, electronic or mechanical, including photocopying, taping and recording, without prior written permission from the publisher. • British Library Cataloguing in Publication Data: a catalogue record for this book is available from the British Library • ISBN 978-1-4063-7643-2 • www.walker.co.uk • 10 9 8 7 6 5 4 3 2 1

WALKER BOOKS
AND SUBSIDIARIES
LONDON • BOSTON • SYDNEY • AUCKLAND

There are certain things
that all little duckies must do every day –

eat their dinner (seeds and berries),

preen themselves clean (with beaks and bubbles),

and go to bed (all in a row).

Little Flo did not do ANY of these things.

She liked to eat naughty treats ...

chase frogs
through mucky puddles ...

and she ALWAYS hid at bedtime.

FLO!

One day, Daddy Duck and Flo were off to visit Auntie Jenna's new nest. Daddy Duck puffed up his feathery chest and said, in his most serious deep duckie voice:

"Now then, Flo. You have to FOLLOW ME all the way. No chasing or hiding, or you'll get lost."

"Yes, Daddy, I promise,"
said Little Flo.

So off they went.

"Why don't we sing a song
as you follow along?" said Daddy.
"I LOVE singing, Daddy," said Flo.
"I can sing VERY high
and VERY LOUD."

"OK, Flo, but listen to me first...

We're off to somewhere new.
So stick to me like glue...

FOLLOW ME, FLO!

Come on, let's go!
We're sure to be
there soon.

Follow me UP...

Follow me DOWN...

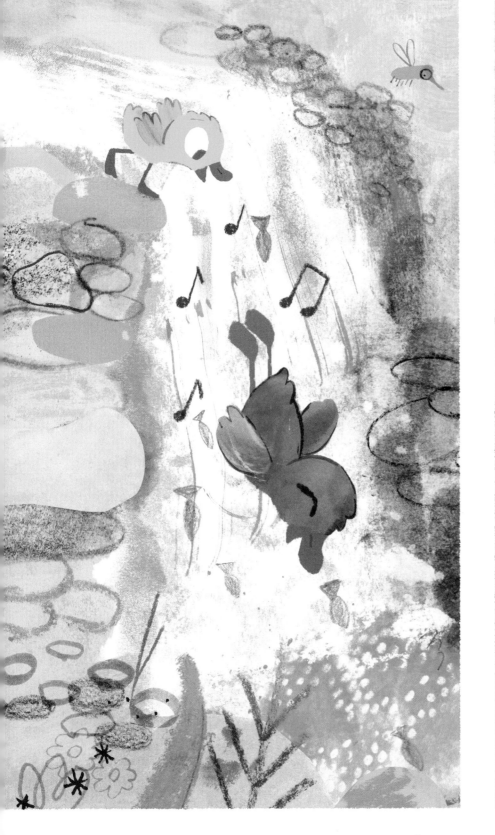

**_Look straight ahead,
and
NOT AROUND!_**

Follow me IN...

Follow me OUT...

If you fall behind,
just give me a
SHOUT!
Yes, follow me,
follow me, Flo..."

Flo thought Daddy's song was all right,
but he didn't sing VERY high or VERY LOUD,
the way that she liked.

So Flo made up her OWN song...

"Follow, follow, follow me,
I'm little duckie
FLO!

Follow, follow, follow me,

I'M SUPER-FAST, NOT SLOW.

UNDER...

OVER...

FUNFAIR

ROUND...

WIN
PRIZES

AND **ROUND**...

UP **HIGH**...

AND WAY DOWN **LOW**.

Now, Flo was SO carried away
singing her new song,
she didn't notice that she
WAS being followed –
and Roxy Fox definitely didn't
want a sing-along!

GRRRRRRR!

QUAAACK!

Oh, golly,
Flo didn't like this AT ALL.
"I want my daddy!"

But Flo had lost sight of Dad
a long time ago.

Then, suddenly, she remembered ...
Daddy's song!
Quickly, she sang:

"*Follow me UP...*

Follow me DOWN...

Look straight ahead, and NOT AROUND!

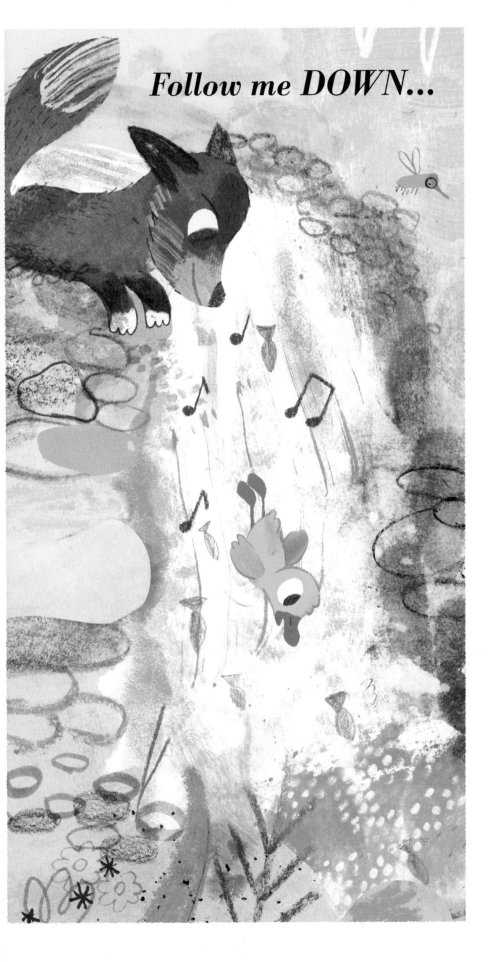

If you fall behind,
just give me
a shout...

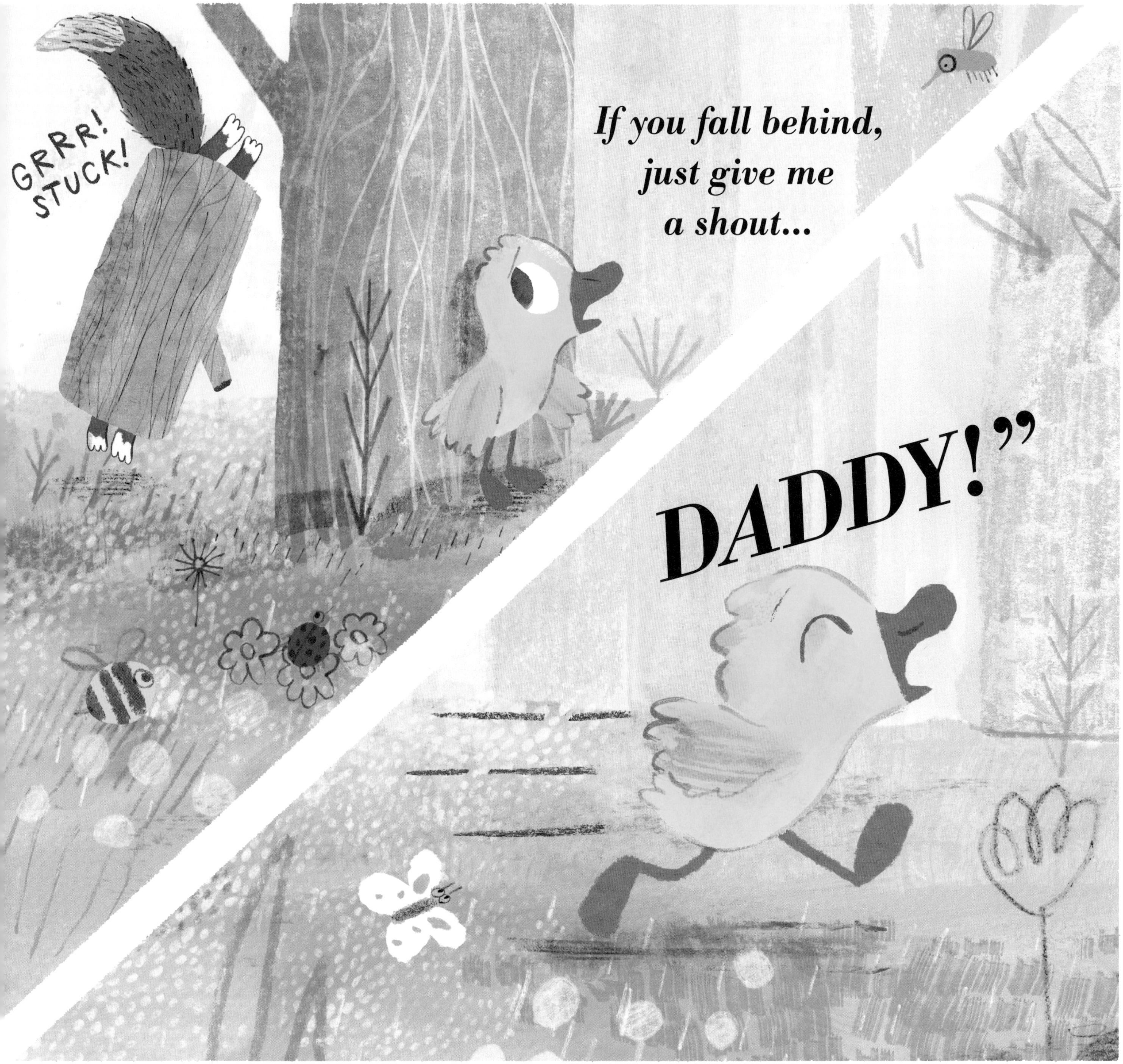

DADDY!"

"Keep up, Flo! Very good following.
We're almost there," said Daddy Duck.

"I LOVE your Follow Song, Daddy," said Flo.
"It's my absolute favourite in the whole world."

And when they got to Auntie Jenna's new home,

oh, what a happy,
dizzy, duckie dance
they all had!

That night, Flo ate all of her seeds and berries
(like a good little duckie),

preened herself squeaky-clean (for the very first time),

and fell fast asleep (perfectly in a row).

And the next morning,
for being SO good at following on the way over,
Daddy Duck let Flo lead the way home...

*"Follow, follow, follow me,
I'm little duckie
FLO!"*

QUAAACK!